GROWN-UPS ARE DUMB!

(NO OFFENSE)

By Alexa Kitchen

(The World's Youngest Professional Cartoonist)

𝒟𝒾𝓈𝓃𝑒𝓎 🐱 HYPERION BOOKS

NEW YORK

W

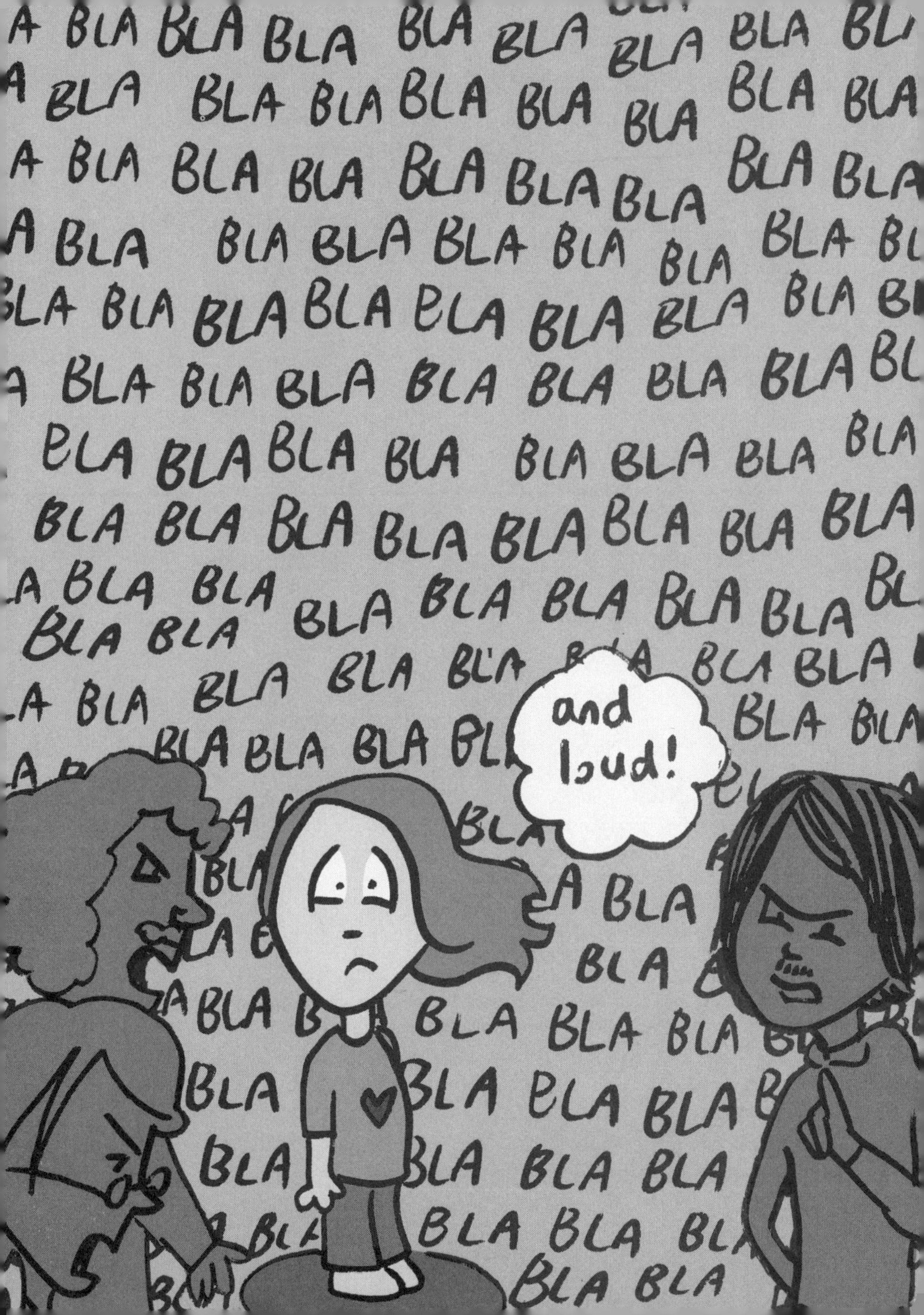
and loud!

I'd like to thank my Mom for always being there for me and Dad for not butting in with dumb changes. Thank you to John Lind for designing another one of my books so nicely, and Bryant Johnson for helping with the cool pink colors. Thanks also to my editor, Tamson Weston (no offense on that Molly editor joke!), and Nellie Kurtzman, who I know will sell a zillion copies. And Henry Dunow too, for whatever exactly agents do. And Ava, my precious pup. That's it.

Printed in the United States of America

First Edition
10 9 8 7 6 5 4 3 2 1
Library of Congress Cataloging-in-Publication Data on file.
Reinforced binding
ISBN 978-1-4231-1331-7
Visit www.hyperionbooksforchildren.com

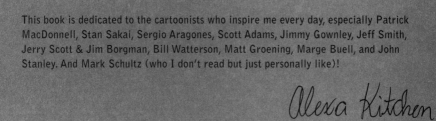

This book is dedicated to the cartoonists who inspire me every day, especially Patrick MacDonnell, Stan Sakai, Sergio Aragones, Scott Adams, Jimmy Gownley, Jeff Smith, Jerry Scott & Jim Borgman, Bill Watterson, Matt Groening, Marge Buell, and John Stanley. And Mark Schultz (who I don't read but just personally like)!

Alexa Kitchen

"That Molly Kid"   Alexa Kitchen

MATH

ENGLISH

HISTORY

LIBRARY

SOCIAL STUDIES

WRITING

ART

MUSIC

DISMISSAL

"That Molly kid" — Alexa Kitchen

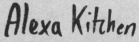

"That Molly kid"   Alexa Kitchen

"That Molly kid" Alexa Kitchen

CAT CHART

SOUND	TRANSLATION
MEEOOOW!!	I am sooo hungry, so feed me *NOW!*
MEW?	Snuggle time! I crave *LOVE!!*
FFFFTTT!	Quit it *NOW,* or you're human mush!
HISSss!	I do NOT want attention!
MEOW!	What's up?

STEP ONE

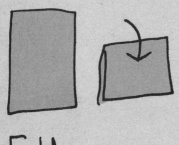

Fold in
half.

STEP THREE

Fold upside down until
the corners have been
tucked under the corners,
which you should then
fold at similar angles
to a random corner
angle.

STEP FOUR

Switch angles of the 73.0998 degree angle parallel to the southwest corner-fold neatly at the edges and tuck in the corners. You have a star!

Filthy Forever
Alexa Kitchen
MOM
DAD
RED SOX
WIND FORCE
KILLS 90.9 OF GERMS
DOESN'T BLEACH OR STAIN
$3.75
ROCK
KIDS— CLEAN YOUR CLOSET OUT ON MONDAY -MOM
MUSIC
LUV
ORANGE
CANDY
HI, HIPPO
LOOK
M&M'S
WHERE'S WALDO?
Crayola
AMY
"HELLO" said bunny. "HELLO" said kitty. Bunny went along, singing.
THE GOBLIN WAS SHOCKED. "RUN AWAY!" HE SCREAMED.

- ART -

BOOK

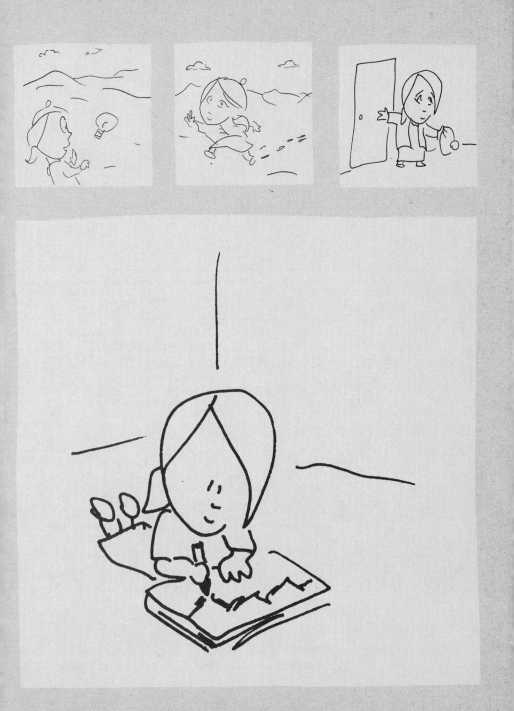

NOISE, PENS, and ANNOYING LITTLE BROTHERS

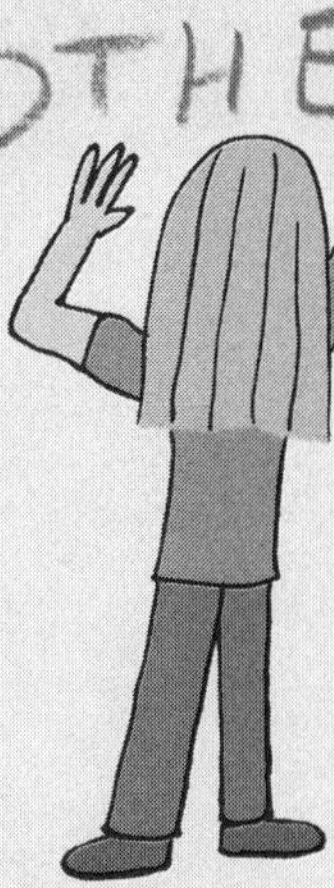

BY

Alexa Kitchen

The great explorer discovers new lands and writes about exotic places.

**From the underwater paradise of the
bright blue sea . . .**

. . . to the mighty kingdom of the
African savanna . . .

. . . to the thick, dense jungles of the Amazon . . .

. . . to the loud, hectic torture chambers
of Lauranville Elementary. . . .

In this habitat, life is tough for day-dreamers.

But the bus is even worse. It's a moving avalanche of noise.

The bus driver's desperate and failing attempt to make the radio drown out the shouting just adds to the noise.

What a day.

What a day.

Joe is like the noise on my school bus multiplied by the number of stars in the sky.

Maybe I can get some peace and quiet upstairs.

YAHOO
HOW TO ANNOY SISTERS
CHEERIOS
MAR-BLES
CLEAN MY ROOM?!
That juice is a month old, but I can't tell her THAT...
I-I-I CAN'T! THAT JUICE IS, WHAT, A WEEK OLD? AND, UH, I-

My black ballpoint pen . . .

. . . my only friend.

I'm a cartoonist, and I get my ideas from daydreaming.

And life's bad times.

My name is Sharon.

SHARON!
TIME TO DO YOUR HOMEWORK!

Homework is the word for frustration, confusion, denial of help, and hate, all rolled into one. It's a curse, a monster, a waste of time. You get the idea.

And finally, when your homework is done . . .

. . . bedtime.

Oh well. At least tomorrow is Friday.

A new day.

Let's hope for the best.

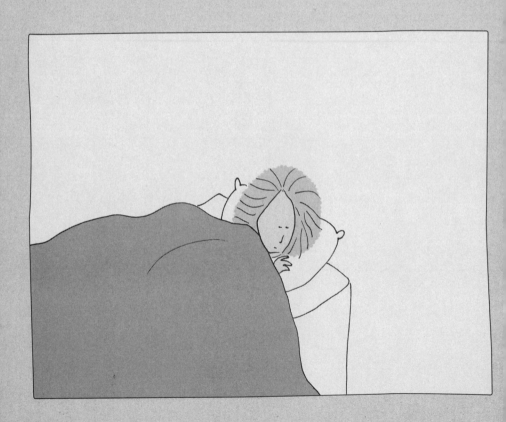

Hurricane
Abby

by Alexa Kitchen

Alexa Kitchen's Hurricane Abby

Alexa Kitchen's HurricaneAbby

Alexa Kitchen's HurricaneAbby

Kathy Ford

and the Boring Friday

by Alexa Kitchen, age 10

Kathy Ford

and the Boring Friday

by Alexa Kitchen ♥

Kathy Ford

and the Boring Friday

by Alexa Kitchen ♥

Kathy Ford
and the Boring Friday

by Alexa Kitchen ♥

Kathy Ford

and the Boring Friday

by Alexa Kitchen ♥

Kathy Ford
and the Boring Friday

by Alexa Kitchen ♥

Kathy Ford

and the Boring Friday

by Alexa Kitchen ♥

Kathy Ford
and the Boring Friday

by Alexa Kitchen ♥

Kathy Ford

MY BROTHER IS BIGFOOT

by Alexa Kitchen, age 10

Kathy Ford
MY BROTHER IS BIGFOOT
by Alexa Kitchen ♥

Kathy Ford

MY BROTHER IS BIGFOOT

by Alexa Kitchen ♥

CLEAN YOUR ROOM!

Look at these MOLDY SOCKS!

THAT'S MY SCIENCE PROJECT!

I'm growing various species of mold for science class! DUH!

This one is ..... uh.... ummm, grossus moldirex!

There are footprints on the ceiling, and toothpaste boogers smeared on the window, and rotten food all over!

Your **dirty laundry** is all over the FLOOR!

Swear words are written on your table!

Kathy Ford

MY BROTHER IS BIGFOOT

by Alexa Kitchen ♥

Why is there pink yogurt on your computer screen?

That's not pink yogurt ... that's what's left of my pet salamander. I put him in the blender.

WHAT IS UNDER YOUR BED!!??

That's from when I put a teddy bear in the microwave.

This is SO gross!!!!!!

I remember... this is the spot where I made plans to make the septic tank blow up.

my Mom is wacko

How can you possibly SURVIVE in here? YUCK!

EW!!!

Kathy Ford

MY BROTHER IS BIGFOOT

by Alexa Kitchen ♥

Kathy Ford

and the ROAD TRIP

by Alexa Kitchen, age 10

Kathy Ford

by Alexa Kitchen ♥

and the ROAD TRIP

Kathy Ford

and the ROAD TRIP

by Alexa Kitchen ♥

Kathy Ford
and the ROAD TRIP
by Alexa Kitchen ♥

Kathy Ford
and the ROAD TRIP
by Alexa Kitchen ♥

Kathy Ford

by Alexa Kitchen ♥

and the ROAD TRIP

LATER...

Siblings

Alexa Kitchen is the world's youngest professional cartoonist. Her *Drawing Comics Is Easy! (Except When It's Hard)*, drawn when she was seven, was nominated for both Eisner and Harvey Awards, making her the youngest nominee ever for either. She has been featured in the *New York Times, Boston Globe,* and *London Sunday Telegraph.* She lives in western Massachusetts with her dog, her mom, and her dad—cited here in order of importance.

Your LIFE follows Your WORDS

RELEASING THE PRAYER OF FAITH

DARLENE BISHOP

Foreword by ROD PARSLEY

1.60
3.20
480.00

#4,762.00
160.00
3 #480.00
3.18
1.80